ANN ARBOR DISTRICT LIBRARY

3162121083800

SO-AZL-592

Picnic!

A Day in the Park

By Joan Holub

Illustrated by Will Terry

Ready-to-Read • Aladdin

New York London Toronto Sydney

For Dia Calhoun,
author and friend –J. H.

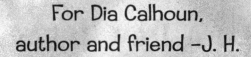

ALADDIN PAPERBACKS
An imprint of Simon & Schuster Children's Publishing Division
1230 Avenue of the Americas, New York, NY 10020
Text copyright © 2008 by Joan Holub
Illustrations copyright © 2008 by Will Terry
All rights reserved, including the right of reproduction in whole or in part in any form.
READY-TO-READ is a registered trademark of Simon & Schuster, Inc.
ALADDIN PAPERBACKS and related logo are registered trademarks of Simon &
Schuster, Inc.
Designed by Lisa Vega
The text of this book was set in font Century Oldstyle BT.
Manufactured in the United States of America
First Aladdin Paperbacks edition June 2008
2 4 6 8 10 9 7 5 3 1
Cataloging-in-Publication Data is on file with
the Library of Congress.
ISBN-13: 978-1-4169-5133-9
ISBN-10: 1-4169-5133-4

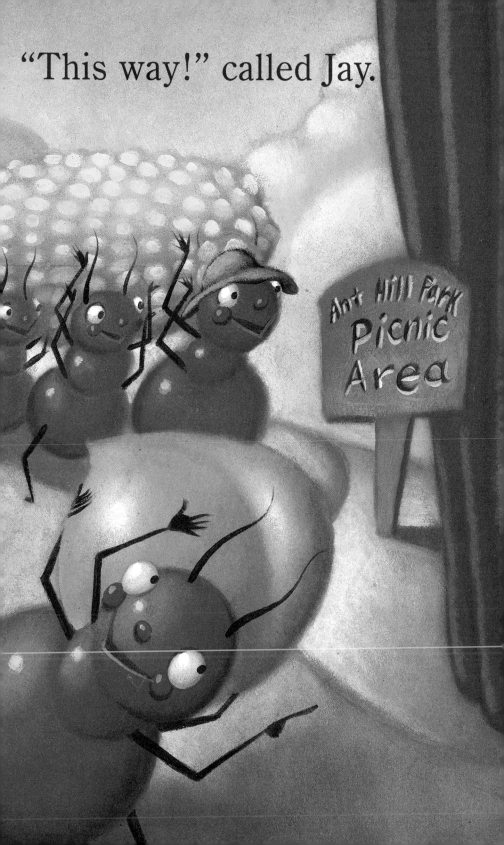

"This way!" called Jay.

"Corn cob," said Rob.

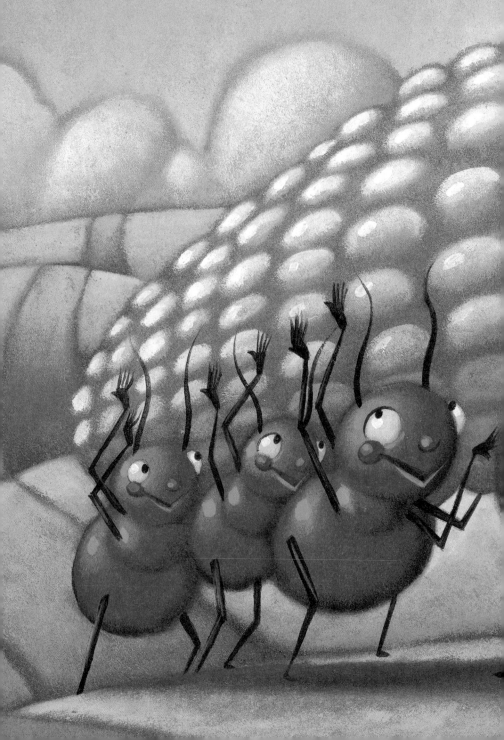

"Watermelon,"
said Helen.

"A bean," said Jean.
"A pea," said Dee.

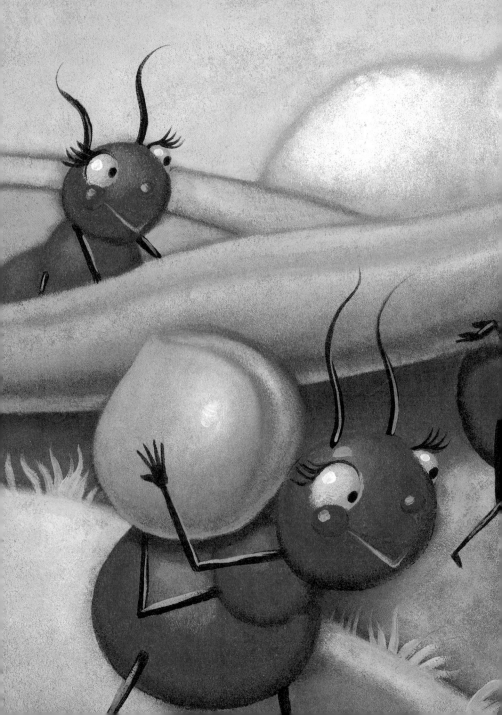

"A roll," said Noel.
"And jam," said Pam.

"And pie!" said Guy.

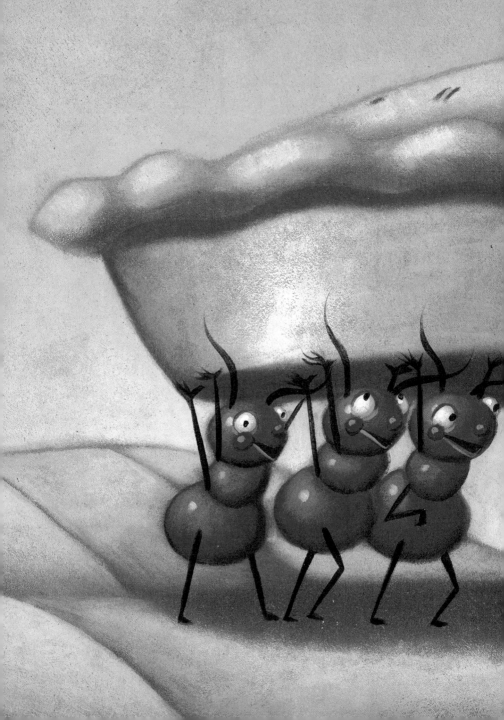

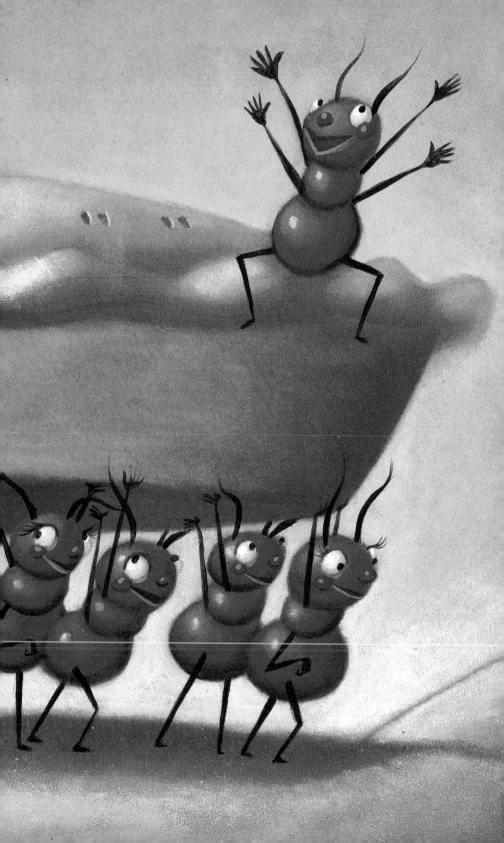

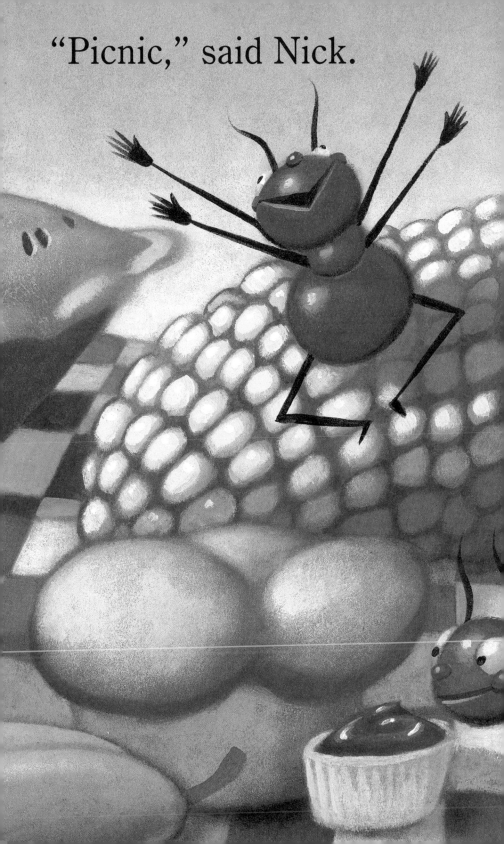

"Picnic," said Nick.

"All gone," said Dawn.

"Time to go," said Joe.

"Which way?" asked Jay.
"Don't know," said Joe.

"Can't see," said Dee.
"Too dark," said Clark.

Blink, blink,
went Link.

Flash, flash, went Nash.

"This way!"
said Jay.

"Thank you,"
called Drew.

"Good night," said Dwight.